OLD TOM'S HOLIDAY

Leigh HOBBS

Ω

PEACHTREE

ATLANTA

Angela Throgmorton loved Old Tom, but caring for him was hard work.
He liked to relax, and he never helped around the house.

One morning, Angela received some exciting news.
She had won a luxury holiday trip! Angela was thrilled.
And so was Old Tom. He was *always* in the mood for a vacation.

Angela finished the dishes and then packed her bags…

…and Old Tom packed his.

But just when he was ready to leave, Old Tom heard some dreadful news.
"It's a trip for one," said Angela Throgmorton. "Why don't you clean
your room while I'm gone?"

Soon Angela was on her way.

She was upset to be leaving Old Tom, of course.

"But there's food in the freezer and I won't be gone for long," Angela told herself.
She settled back and studied her travel brochures.

On her first night away, Angela stayed in a lovely hotel.
"I'm sure I folded these more carefully," she said, as she
unpacked a few of her favorite things.

In the morning, Angela was amazed by all the skyscrapers!
She wanted to blend in, so she had her hair done just right.

Angela was on the move
all the time.

She caught trains

and flew in planes.

She sailed on ships

and was chauffeured in cars.

Angela rode on buses too.

She didn't want to miss a thing.

At a museum she admired an ancient pot.
"What beautiful creatures they had back then," said Angela.

While picnicking in the gardens of a royal palace,
something made her think of her own garden far away.

Angela was glad that she had bought a new camera for her trip.

She wanted to photograph the interesting wildlife.

"I can't wait to show my photos to Old Tom," she said.

Angela visited an art gallery, where she saw a painting
that reminded her of home.

While on a tour of the desert, Angela thought she saw Old Tom.
"It must be a mirage," she sighed, a little disappointed.

Angela had afternoon tea in an exclusive cafe.
But when Old Tom's favorite cakes arrived,
she wondered if tea for two might have been more fun.

By now, Angela was exhausted from all her traveling.
At a concert one night, she was so sleepy that she missed
the appearance of a surprise guest performer.

Then later, while strolling back to her hotel,
Angela was bewitched by a beautiful moon.

The following afternoon,
Angela noticed an unusual sunset.

She ought to have been having a wonderful time,
but something was missing.
"Old Tom is everywhere I look!" cried Angela,
as she ran to her room.

Angela was lonely.

So she picked up the phone and called Old Tom. But no one was home.
"He's out having fun," sobbed Angela. "Where could he be?"

At that very moment, a furry shape fell into her lap.
"Oh, my baby! What a wonderful surprise!"
Angela knew better than to ask any questions.

Instead, it was time to celebrate.

So she took Old Tom to a fancy restaurant.

"Order whatever you want!" said Angela Throgmorton.

And that is just what Old Tom did.
His table manners hadn't improved at all.
But for once Angela didn't mind…

…now that this was a holiday for two.

For David Francis and Julia Murray

Ω

Published by
PEACHTREE PUBLISHERS, LTD.
1700 Chattahoochee Avenue
Atlanta, Georgia 30318-2112
www.peachtree-online.com

ISBN 1-56145-316-1

Text and illustrations © 2002 by Leigh Hobbs

First published in Australia by ABC books in 2002

10 9 8 7 6 5 4 3 2 1
First Edition

Illustrations created in pen, ink, gouache, and acrylic

Printed in China

Library of Congress Cataloging-in-Publication Data

Hobbs, Leigh.
Old Tom's holiday / written and illustrated by Leigh Hobbs.-- 1st ed.
p. cm.
Summary: Angela goes off on a vacation that she has won,
but is surprised to find that everything reminds her of the cat
she thought she left at home.
ISBN 1-56145-316-1
[1. Cats--Fiction. 2. Vacations--Fiction.] I. Title.

PZ7.H65236Ol 2004
[E]--dc22
2003023530